For Marti and Cy

Over two thousand years ago in ancient Greece
there was a slave called Aesop who loved telling stories.
Aesop told more than two hundred fables and
here are six of them in modern versions.

•

First published in the United States by Dial Books for Young Readers
2 Park Avenue · New York, New York 10016
Published in Canada by Fitzhenry & Whiteside Limited, Toronto
Published in Great Britain by Andersen Press Ltd.
Copyright © 1986 by Tony Ross
All rights reserved
Printed in Italy
Design by Sara Reynolds
First Edition
C O B E
2 4 6 8 10 9 7 5 3 1

Library of Congress Cataloging-in-Publication Data
Ross, Tony. Foxy fables.
Summary: Contemporary retellings of six fables from Aesop,
including "The Fox and the Crow," "The Stag and his
Mirrors," and "The Hare and the Tortoise."
1. Fables. [1. Fables] I. Title.
PZ8.2.R67Fo 1986 [E] [398.2] 85-27436
ISBN 0-8037-0291-4

The art for each picture consists of a black ink and
watercolor painting, which is camera-separated
and reproduced in full color.

FOXY FABLES

· TONY ROSS ·

Dial Books for Young Readers

NEW YORK

THE FOX AND THE CROW

Madame Crow was very large and glossy black. When she was a small crowlet, someone told her that she had a lovely voice (for a crow), and ever since then she had fancied herself an opera singer. She was an unbearable crow.

She would strut around town, feeling more important than everyone else, and close her eyes, throw her head back, and screech. She didn't see everyone running away with their hands over their ears. Madame Crow was a real pain.

One day Madame Crow was walking around the market when she spied a cheese stall. She stared at the wonderful cheeses on display: Cheddar, mozzarella, blue ones, red ones, foreign ones . . . . They looked yummy! "I-I-I-I-I thinnnnnnk I'll haaaaaave a piece of cheddar!" Madame Crow sang to a theme from "Madame Butterfly." And she just helped herself to a beakful.

"Hey, you!" shouted the stall keeper. "Aren't you going to pay for that?"

"Let her have it," yelled all the other customers. "It'll keep her beak shut."

Madame Crow ignored everybody and hopped away with her piece of cheese. She went straight home and sat by the window, watching the world and hoping the world would watch her. She held the cheese firmly in her beak.

Just then a poor fox strolled by. He was very hungry. "That's a tasty piece of cheese," he thought as he stopped and looked up at Madame Crow.

"Gracious!" he gasped. "What a fine bird!"

Madame Crow glanced down and smiled mysteriously.

"Such obvious breeding, such beauty!"

Madame Crow wriggled with delight.

"Those flashing eyes, those slender, blue-black quills…"

Madame Crow peered down at the fox, waiting for more compliments.

"Perhaps he is unaware of my exceptionally fine voice," she thought. Madame Crow leaned out of her window and tried to impress the fox with a couple of verses of "Tiptoe Through the Tulips."

As she opened her beak to sing, the cheese fell out … down to the street below.

The fox grabbed the cheese and gobbled it up. "Exquisite!" he said, and went on his way.

THE CAT AND THE FOX

One day the fox was taking a walk in the park when he met the most beautiful cat he had ever seen. She was smaller than the fox, but not very much. Her nose was shorter, but not very much. Her tail was thinner, but not very much. All in all she looked enough like the fox for him to fall in love with her.

The cat, however, didn't think much of the fox. She thought that he was sort of a show-off, and anyway, she didn't like redheads. Soon the fox found out where the cat lived, and he hung around every day hoping to see her. Whenever she stepped out of her front door, the fox would spring forward, take her paw, and walk with her. The cat was much too polite to tell the fox to get lost; after all, she was purebred.

The fox liked to talk about himself all the time. "I've got a boat on the river!" he said.

"Indeed?" replied the cat, smiling. "I hate water!"

"I drink whiskey with no ice!" smirked the fox. "Would you like some?"

"Gracious no!" said the cat, smiling. "I prefer milk."

"I know a thousand and one tricks," giggled the fox. "How many do you know?"

The cat struggled to remember her manners and not use rude words with this dumb, bushy-tailed nitwit. "How clever!" She yawned. "I only know *one*."

Their walk had taken the two animals into the rough part of town, and they ran into a gang of wolves and mean dogs, all stretched out across the pavement. The cat shot up the nearest tree.

The fox tried his thousand and one tricks. He tried judo and karate, but the gang just punched his nose. He tried telling jokes, but the gang didn't understand them and boxed his ears. He tried to argue, but the gang wouldn't listen. It was more fun to kick the fox up into the air. Dumbest of all, he tried to fight back and bit a mean dog's tail. Enraged, the mean dog swung the fox into the air and slammed him against the pavement. Then, tiring of their game, the nasty gang left.

The badly battered fox looked up into the tree where the cat sat safely. "So what's your one trick?" he snarled.

"I can climb trees," she purred.

THE FOX AND THE GOAT

One hot day there were some *terrible* smells drifting around the Foxes' house. Mr. Fox didn't mind too much, but Mrs. Fox did. She looked everywhere to find the cause of the awful smells. Mr. Fox watched TV. At last the trouble was found – the drains were blocked.

Mrs. Fox said to her husband, "Unless you do something about those drains, I will call the plumber and that will cost you a lot of money."

"Then I'll do it right away," said Mr. Fox. He jumped up, found his

brush and flashlight, and went into the street. He hopped down the
manhole and landed with a splash in two feet of dirty water. The
smell was even worse down there.

Mr. Fox tried to clear the drain, but he couldn't — he'd left his
brush on the street. "I'll have to go and get my tools!" he muttered
angrily, and then, to his horror, he found that he couldn't climb out
of the drain. The walls were too deep and slippery. The silly fox
hadn't thought of bringing a ladder. So he sat in the smelly water,
slapping himself on the nose, and telling himself what a dumbbell
he'd been.

Suddenly a voice came from above. "Hello!"

Mr. Fox looked up. It was the crazy old goat from across the street.
"What are you doing down there?" asked the goat.

"Relaxing in the water," said Mr. Fox. "You know, a health spa."

"Doesn't smell too good," said the goat, who wasn't *that* crazy.
"No," agreed Mr. Fox, "but then, things that are good for you are often pretty nasty, aren't they?"

The goat thought about all the medicine he'd ever taken. "Yes," he said. "Mind if I come down and share your cure?"

"Be my guest," grinned Mr. Fox. "There's enough smelly water for both of us."

So the crazy goat jumped down into the drain too. As soon as he did, Mr. Fox used his horns as a ladder and scrambled up onto the street.

"I don't like it here," cried the goat. "How do I get out?"

"I'll go and get a ladder," said Mr. Fox, grinning as he threw his brush down. "It'll take some time, so while I'm gone, you might as well clear that drain!"

THE FOX AND THE STORK

The fox loved to eat out, but since it was so expensive, nobody would go with him. And the fox *hated* to eat alone.

One evening he ran into his friend the stork. "How about dinner in a nice café?" said the fox, trotting after him.

"Oh, dear, no," said the stork. "I can't afford it."

"Please come," pleaded the fox. "I really love to hear your stories and I'll pay."

"Well, okay," sighed the stork. He did feel very hungry.

When the two friends arrived at the café, the stork was ravenous. The head waiter handed the menu to the fox. "I'll order for us. Asparagus soup, please, for my friend and me."

The soup was served in shallow soup dishes, and while the fox was able to lap his up with relish, the stork couldn't eat — his long thin beak was useless with the wide, shallow dish. "Not hungry?" sniggered the fox. "Don't worry, I'll find room for yours." And so the crafty fox got to eat *both* bowls of soup at no extra cost.

The stork sat back and looked around. "A nice place," he said, "but I know a better one. Do you want to go there for dessert?"

"Why not," said the fox, smiling. "We'll top off a great evening with a delicious dessert."

The head waiter at the next café seemed to know the stork. "Good evening, sir," he said. "A table for two?"

"Near the door," said the stork. They sat down and the stork took the menu before the fox could get his paws on it. "Two Knicker-bocker glories," he ordered.

They were ice cream with candies, served in the tallest, thinnest glasses the fox had ever seen. The fox could only get his snout into the very top of the glass, but the stork could sink his long beak right down to the bottom. After finishing every drop, the stork looked at the fox who was still struggling to get his fat nose into the long thin glass. "Not hungry?" The stork smiled and taking the glass from the fox he gobbled down all the ice cream.

The waiter came by. "Is everything all right?" he asked.

"Yes, thank you," said the stork. "My friend is paying." And with that, he slipped quickly out of the door.

THE STAG AND HIS MIRRORS

Astag had just moved into an apartment. He went to a big store and bought some chairs, a TV, and a video recorder. Still the apartment needed *something*. Ah, that was it! The walls were bare!

The stag ran back to the store and asked to see some paintings. The salesman showed him lots — all with stags standing on hills. "Don't you have anything more...well...cheerful?" said the stag.

"No more paintings," said the salesman, "but you are such a handsome guy, have you considered a mirror?"

"Handsome guy," thought the stag. "I'll take one!" he said.

The salesman didn't think the stag was particularly handsome, but at least he'd made a sale.

The stag hung his mirror over the fireplace. "I certainly am handsome," he said. "Look at the graceful curve of those horns!"

The stag admired his horns every day, and as time went by he hung mirrors on all his walls so he could see his handsome horns wherever he looked.

"Now I must buy a *big* mirror to stand on the floor," thought the vain animal as he hurried back to the department store.

The salesman showed him a beautiful long mirror, and the stag stepped back to admire himself. What a shock he got! In the smaller mirrors he had only seen his head and shoulders. Now he could see *all* of himself...those wonderful horns...and...oh, dear...those dopey, spindly, thin, funny-looking, hairy, awful little legs.

The stag refused to buy the mirror and rushed out of the department store.

Outside he ran...bump...into a gang of uncouth wolves back from a football game. "Get him!" they screamed, pointing at the stag.

The stag ran off and his dopey, spindly, thin, funny-looking, hairy, awful little legs allowed him to escape from the wolves. He ran much faster than any of them...

and only stopped when he spied his reflection in a shop window on the corner. How handsome his horns looked...but, wait, they were tangled in the overhead trolley wires...

and a trolley car was coming.

THE HARE AND THE TORTOISE

One night the Hare was having a quiet drink with the Tortoise, and as usual the conversation turned to sports. Also as usual the Hare was bragging about how good he was at shuffleboard, croquet, darts...everything. As he spoke he kept poking the Tortoise on the shell. At last the Tortoise snapped, "You may be okay at all the *easy* sports, but I'm a better *athlete* than you."

The bar suddenly got quiet. The Tortoise wished he'd kept his big mouth shut. The Hare couldn't believe his long ears. "*Running*, you mean?" he said.

"Running!" gulped the Tortoise. "Maybe you're a great bowler, but I'm the better runner." And so a race was arranged for the next day. The Tortoise went home to bed wondering why he ever said such ridiculous things.

The following day a two-mile course was marked out by the Mole. The Hare and the Tortoise took off their sweatsuits and went to the starting line. The Mole pointed his pistol into the air and pulled the trigger. The Hare shot off as if he'd been stung. As he went around the first bend, the Tortoise was still trying to get his feet out of the starting blocks.

After the first mile the Hare stopped and looked back. He couldn't even see the Tortoise. "This is no fun," he muttered. "I want the Tortoise to *see* me win. I'll wait here while he catches up." Having decided this, the Hare sat under a tree and fell asleep in the sun.

Twenty minutes later the Tortoise came plodding along, wheezing badly. The Hare sat up and waved as the Tortoise creaked past. "Time to go!" laughed the Hare, and he leaped up. What he didn't notice was the low branch just above his head, and he crashed his dumb head into it, knocking himself out.

The Tortoise plodded on toward the finish line. When the Hare regained his senses, he hurried toward the finish, but it was too late. The Tortoise had already crossed the line, was wearing the gold-plated medal, and was doing push-ups.

As the hot and angry Hare crossed the line to the jeers of the crowd, the Tortoise looked up.

"Any good at highjumping?" he said, grinning.